P9-DDR-093

For Dr. Alisa Peet and Barbara Benioff Friedman,
two of the great Jewish mothers of all time. —A.P.

For my mother, whose Christmases would
have made anyone jealous. —A.T.

For Sylvie Bunelle-Weill, my dear friend. —C.D.

A portion of the authors' proceeds from the sale of this book are donated to
Seeds of Peace, a non-profit organization founded in 1993 as a leadership and
peace-building program for Palestinian, Israeli, and Egyptian teenagers. The program
has since expanded to include young leaders from areas of conflict around the world.

Text copyright © 2015 by Amanda Peet and Andrea Troyer
Jacket art and interior illustrations copyright © 2015 by Christine Davenier

All rights reserved. Published in the United States by Doubleday, an imprint of Random House Children's Books,
a division of Random House LLC, a Penguin Random House Company, New York.

Doubleday and the colophon are registered trademarks of Random House LLC.

Visit us on the Web! randomhousekids.com

Educators and librarians, for a variety of teaching tools, visit us at RHTeachersLibrarians.com

Library of Congress Cataloging-in-Publication Data
Peet, Amanda, author.
Dear Santa, Love, Rachel Rosenstein / by Amanda Peet and Andrea Troyer ; illustrated by Christine Davenier. —
First edition.
pages cm.
Summary: "A Jewish girl decides that she wants to celebrate Christmas, so she writes a letter to Santa."
—Provided by publisher.
ISBN 978-0-553-51061-4 (trade) — ISBN 978-0-553-51062-1 (lib. bdg.) — ISBN 978-0-553-51063-8 (ebook)
[1. Christmas—Fiction. 2. Santa Claus—Fiction. 3. Jews—United States—Fiction.] I. Troyer, Andrea, author.
II. Davenier, Christine, illustrator. III. Title.
PZ7.1.P44De 2015 [E]—dc23 2014029948

MANUFACTURED IN CHINA
10 9 8 7 6 5 4 3 2 1
First Edition

Random House Children's Books supports the First Amendment and celebrates the right to read.

Dear Santa, Love, Rachel Rosenstein

written by **Amanda Peet** and **Andrea Troyer**

illustrated by **Christine Davenier**

Doubleday Books for Young Readers

Rachel Rosenstein loved Christmas.

She loved the thousand twinkly lights that went up in her neighborhood, the gi-normous Christmas tree in the town square, and the store windows crowded with Santas, elves, candy canes, glittery tinsel, and piles and piles of presents wrapped in shiny, beautiful paper.

Everyone on her block celebrated Christmas. . . .

Everyone except for Rachel Rosenstein.

The Rosensteins didn't celebrate Christmas because
they were Jewish.

Being Jewish was fun *most* of the time.

It meant you got to hunt for the afikomen on Passover,

blow the shofar on Rosh Hashanah,

and get a present a
day for all eight days
of Hanukkah—not to
mention as many latkes
as you could eat.

It meant that when they celebrated Shabbat, Rachel and
her friends and family passed around the challah and said
the same blessings that Papa Murray said as a child. And his
papa before that. And his papa before that. And on and on
until Rachel's head began to spin.

But when Christmas came to town . . .

. . . Rachel felt like a kid in a candy store with no mouth.

"Can we please put up some lights this year?" she asked, staring out the window at her best friend Tina's house.

"No," said her mom.

"How about a tree? Emily Berenbaum's family has a tree and they're Jewish."

"You can't sit on two horses with one behind," said Papa Murray.

"I can," said her mom. "Especially after that meal."

That night, Rachel wrote a secret letter.

Dear Santa

I live in the brick house on Huntley Drive.
YES the one with NO holiday decorations.
It ~~does~~ does have a chimney and there will
be cookies waiting if you come down it.
I've been really good all year and I know
that you are a fair person and will
not mind that I am Jewish. After all
so was Jesus, at least on his mother's side.
LOVe,
Rachel Rosenstein

"Christmas is in less than a week." Rachel looked up to find
her sister Hannah hanging off the top bunk. "There's no way that
letter's going to get to the North Pole in time."

Hannah had a point.

As luck would have it, a couple of days later, Tina's mom asked if Rachel would like to tag along to see Santa at the mall.

"Did you get my letter?" Rachel asked when it was her turn.

"I sure did," said Santa. "Remind me what it said."

"Are you coming to my house even though I'm Jewish?"

"Time for a picture!" said an elf. Click! Click! FLASH!
For a moment, Rachel couldn't see. The next thing she knew,
someone else was on Santa's lap.

Now Christmas was only one day away.
Santa was going to skip over Rachel's house
unless she did something radical.

There was just one thing missing: cookies for Santa.
In the kitchen there were no cookies, only leftover latkes.
Rachel pressed some chocolate chips into them and tried
one. It was good. Better than good. She ate three more
and put the last one out for Santa with a glass of milk.

The Rosensteins were ready for Christmas

Rachel stayed awake as long as she could, lying in her bed listening for the clip-clop of Santa's reindeer on the roof. Visions of sugarplum fairies danced in her head.

But the next morning . . .

"AAAAAGGGGHHH!!!"

There were no piles of presents. "My shirt!"
Hannah cried. "What did you do to my favorite shirt?!"
"Hey, what's all the commotion?" asked Mom.
"CHRISTMAS IS STUPID AND SO IS RACHEL!"
yelled Hannah.

Rachel cried. Across the street, she could see Tina's family in their pajamas, opening the presents Santa had brought for them.

Her mom sat down next to her. "Sometimes, no matter how badly we want something, we just have to accept what is. Okay? I gotta get to work."

"Nobody else's mom works on Christmas," Rachel said.

"Just because it's Christmas doesn't mean there aren't sick kids at the hospital. The world doesn't stop."

Rachel cleaned up her mess.

Later that afternoon, her dad took them
to the park, which was practically empty.

And for dinner, they took Papa Murray to the Chinese place they went to every Christmas. Papa Murray ate chicken feet that looked *exactly* like chicken feet. Rachel's dad stuck chopsticks up his nose like a walrus. "Don't try this at home."

Rachel tried to eat her favorite salty dumplings, but she was too sad.

Then she saw some familiar faces: Lucy Deng from her class, and Mike Rashid and Amina Singh.

"What are you guys doing here?"

"We don't celebrate Christmas, and this is the only place that's open," said Mike.

"You celebrate Hanukkah too?"

"No," said Lucy, "but Chinese New Year is in a few weeks."

Amina said, "We celebrate Diwali. It's the festival of lights."

"Hanukkah's the festival of lights!" said Rachel.

"I celebrate my BIRTHDAY!!!" said Lucy's little sister.

The older kids laughed. "That doesn't count. Everyone does that."

And Rachel realized: when there were so many great holidays in the world, why feel so bad about one little old day like Christmas?

Well, maybe she could feel a *tiny* bit bad.